GAMEDAY!

Winning With Sportsmanship:
The Gary Goodsport Story

JEFF ECKERT

GAMEDAY!
Winning With Sportsmanship:
The Gary Goodsport Story

Copyright © 2023 by JLE Publications, LLC

Editing by Mary-Lane Kamberg
Illustrations by Anedios
Interior Design by Spoonbridge Press

ISBN 978-1-73523-911-8
Printed in the United States of America
First Printing, 2023
24 23 22 21 20 5 4 3 2 1

To order, visit jeckertbooks.com or go to Amazon.com. The nationally endorsed adult companion book, #Sportsmanship: Go Viral With It!, is also available at Amazon.

Praise for

GAMEDAY! Winning With Sportsmanship: The Gary Goodsport Story

"The words and graphics in this book tell a powerful story with the emphasis on fair play and being a good sport. This is especially noteworthy when it comes to accepting what a referee does when the call does not go "your way." That is a key lesson for life. Sports is simply life with the volume turned up. That mantra helps explain many of the things we unfortunately witness at sporting events, especially at the youth levels. This is a very fine piece of work."

—**Barry Mano, President, National Association of Sports Officials**

"I don't know many people who have officiated more games than Jeff. Across all sports, he has seen it all in one form or the other. GAMEDAY! is the result of his vast experience. Everyone can benefit from his encouragement. One of my friends, Robert Block MD and one-time President of the American Academy of Pediatrics, once said in a speech, "All adults were once children." He was speaking about the importance of play and how important it is in early childhood development. GAMEDAY! emphasizes the importance of showing, teaching, and demonstrating good sportsmanship to our kids for their future success. After nearly every speaking engagement with my book, "Keepers of the Sandlot", someone will come up to me and say, "Let me tell you about..." It's always about someone who helped them along the way, or someone who didn't. We are role models whether we like it or not. Every message we send is received. GAMEDAY! is a wonderful example of the many lessons that are learned by everyone in the heat of the competition. Jeff is faithfully sharing his experience so we can all be great leaders and good sports. Enjoy GAMEDAY!, it's why we practice!"

—**Bill Severns, former professional baseball player and author of Keepers of the Sandlot"**

What Is Sportsmanship?

SPORTSMANSHIP:

Conduct becoming to a sportsman and involving fair honest rivalry, courteous relations, and graceful acceptance of results.[1]

<hr />

[1] Merriam-Webster Unabridged, s.v. "sportsmanship (n.)," accessed May 1, 2020, https://unabridged.merriam-webster.com/unabridged/sportsmanship.

A Lesson for Parents

This story was written in part by artificial intelligence, or AI. I gave it a few parameters and it added its version of the definition of sportsmanship, the importance of it, and how that would play out in the story of a youth game. Amazing, isn't it!? If artificial intelligence knows what sportsmanship is, I think deep down all of us in the stands and coaching on the sidelines know what it is as well. We just have to choose to embody it for our children. Billy obviously got his attitude from his dad, as did Gary. We are not born with good or bad sportsmanship in our blood. It is a learned behavior. I encourage you to become a sports culture warrior and lead by example.

The adult, nationally acclaimed version of this book, *#Sportsmanship: Go Viral With It!*, is available on Amazon. Go to mybook.to/Sportsmanship or jeckertbooks.com to purchase it.

Jeff Eckert

GAMEDAY!

GARY GOODSPORT BOUNCED DOWN THE STAIRS.

He wore his Blue Eagles basketball uniform. **"Ready, Dad!"** he said. "When are we leaving for the championship game?"

"As soon as I grab my coat," Dad said.

"It is going to be so much fun!"
Gary said.
He loved to play basketball.

"You are playing the
DRAGONS
today," Dad said.

"Oh, no!"
Gary said.

"They always play rough.
I'm a little
nervous."

"If you play hard, you can win," Dad said.

"The referees will call fouls if the Dragons break the rules."

"Your team is awesome. And you have a superpower," his dad said.

"**Superpower?**" Gary asked.

Dad nodded.
"**You are a good sport.**"

"What does that mean?" Gary asked.

"It means you play fair,"
Dad said.

"It means **you treat the other team
and the referees with respect.**

It means
doing your best no matter what.

And it means
**ALWAYS being a polite winner
and a friendly loser."**

The game started, and **the Blue Eagles players cheered for each other.**

The Blue Eagles **parents also cheered** from the stands.

A Dragons player ran down the court. He fell.

Gary held out his hand and helped him up.

Gary's dad smiled in the stands because **he was proud of Gary.**

On the next play, **Billy Badsport pushed a Blue Eagles player**.

The Blue Eagles player **landed on the floor**.

The **referee blew his whistle and called for a foul**, pointing at Billy.

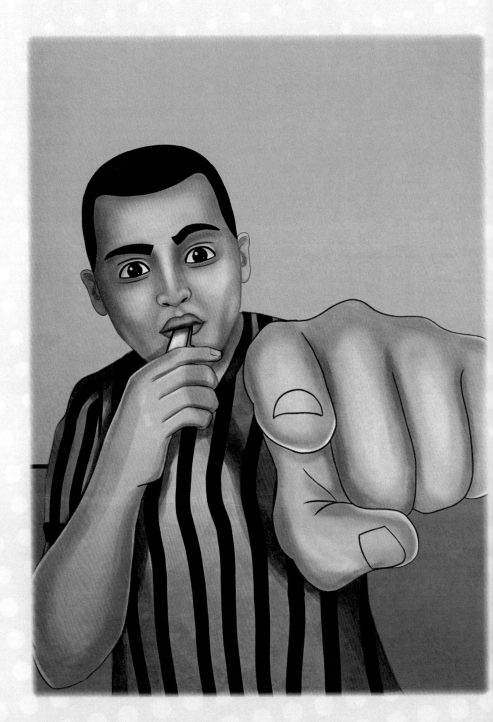

Billy waved his arms in the air.

"I did not foul him," he yelled.

Billy's father also yelled from the stands, "That was not a foul! Come on, ref!"

Other Dragons parents in the stands were embarrassed.

Billy's dad was not being a good sport.

On the very next play, **Gary dribbled down the court.**

He tried to shoot a layup but **Billy stuck out his foot on purpose.**

Gary tripped.

He grabbed his ankle in pain.

Gary's coach knelt next to him.
"Are you OK?" he asked.

"My ankle hurts," Gary said.

Gary wondered if he could keep playing.

His coach helped Gary up and he limped to the bench.

Billy Badsport smiled.

"Good, their best player is hurt!"
he said.

"We will win for sure!"

The Dragons coach called a time-out.

The team **formed a circle** around him.

"I know you boys want to win," he said.

"But you have to show good sportsmanship, too."

The coach looked at Billy.

"Billy, you can't play that way," he said.

"You have to **RESPECT** other players and the referees.

Since you can't do that, **you have to sit out as long as Gary can't play.**"

Billy's dad heard what the coach said.

His face turned red.
"I am sorry for my behavior, too," he said to the Dragon's coach.

"I'll make sure Billy knows **how to be a good sport.**

I will set a good example for him," Billy's Dad said.

The game started again.

The Blue Eagles coach **put in a substitute for Gary.**

The game was fast and the lead changed several times.

Time was running out with only one minute left in the game!

The Dragons **coach called a time-out** with the Blue Eagles leading by two points.

Gary Goodsport told his coach,

"I think I can play the final minute."

The Blue Eagles coach nodded and said,

"OK. Go get 'em!"
and put Gary back in the game.

The Dragons coach saw Gary go back in the game. He looked at Billy.

"Are you going to play fair and be a good sport?" the coach asked.

"Yes sir. I'll do my best," Billy said.

"OK, **you can go back in** to guard Gary," said the coach.

Gary and Billy played great in the last minute!

They **each scored** a basket.

Billy Badsport's dad **cheered for his son**.

He also **clapped when Gary made a basket.**

The game was **exciting and close**.

The Dragons tied the game with just a few seconds left.

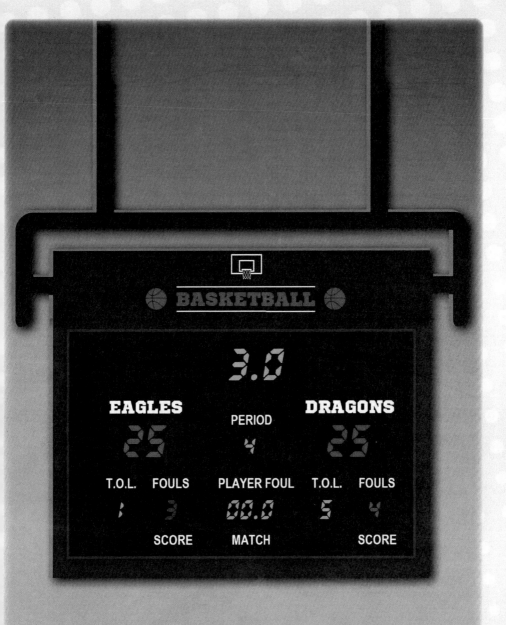

The Blue Eagles inbounded the ball.

Gary Goodsport dribbled hard down the court.

He jumped,

he shot,

and he **made the game-winning basket!**

To his surprise, Billy Badsport came over to him.

Billy shook Gary's hand.

"Great shot!" Billy said.

"You played a great game.
I'm sorry I tripped you."

"You played well, too." Gary said.

"And now you're a good sport too."

The boys went over to the referees and **shook their hands**.

"**Thank you** for refereeing our game," Billy said.

"**You're welcome,**" said one of the referees.

"It is **always fun** for us **when you play fair!**"

Walking out of the gym, Billy's dad put his arm around his son.

"We all like to win, but **sometimes we lose. Win or lose**, we have to **be good sports.**

We both acted much better after your coach talked to us!

I'm **proud** of you. **Give me a high-five!"** Billy's dad said.

The Blue Eagles players were **happy that they won**.

BLUE EAGLES

They were **proud for playing with** good sportsmanship.

They knew they had **made the game fun for everyone**.

The Dragons players also **learned that playing fair was fun**.

They **learned to not complain** about the other team or the referees.

By being **good sports**, the Green Dragons and Blue Eagles made basketball **a better game for everyone**.

Author's Note and Acknowledgments

THIS HAS BEEN A LABOR OF LOVE that allows me to share sportsmanship insights with anyone who can influence a more positive arc, whether a parent, fan, or coach.

Thanks much to my content contributors and reviewers, including Mary-Lane Kamberg, editor, whose skills made this such a fun reading lesson for kids. Thanks to Cory Kiesling, Laura Kiesling, and Janet Eckert for their time spent reviewing the manuscript—several times. And finally, thanks to illustrator Anedios and Spoonbridge Press for their interior design work.

As Gandhi said, you can now be the change you want to see in the world. Good luck, and God bless you on your important journey of raising a good sport and being a sports culture warrior.

Best wishes,
Jeff Eckert
August 2023

About the Author

JEFF ECKERT is a father of three grown children that he coached in baseball, softball, and basketball. His avocation is officiating high school varsity basketball for the last 18 years and, more recently, high school volleyball. He is blessed to have been selected to work 10 postseason high school basketball and volleyball tournaments so far. As a "dad coach" and official, Jeff has seen the best and worst sportsmanship. That is why he is sharing this fictional story and trying to influence a more positive arc in sportsmanship through our youngest generation. You can reach him at jeckertbooks.com.